JOSH DYGERT

STELLA

a novella

STELLA

JOSH DYGERT

Cover by Greg Champman, © 2020 LVP Publications

Stella Copyright © 2020 Josh Dygert, LVP Publications

This is a work of fiction. Names, characters, businesses, places, events and incidents are either the products of the author's imagination or used in a fictitious manner. Any resemblance to actual persons, living or dead, or actual events is purely coincidental.

Lycan Valley Press Publications
1625 E 72nd St STE 700 PMB 132
Tacoma, Washington 98404 United States of America

Printed in the United States of America

First Edition, April 2020

ISBN-978-1-64562-982-5

Stella started as a submission for Lycan Valley's Pulp Horror Book of Phobias. When I saw Kosmikophobia (the fear of cosmic phenomenon) on the list of possible phobias, I just started writing. I want to thank MJae and everyone at Lycan Valley Press Publications for giving me the chance to meet Stella and for shepherding her from short story to novella.

~ 1 ~

I KNEW THE NAMES of the stars and the constellations before I knew my alphabet. My daddy loved the stars, so I loved them too. He told me he met my mom under the influence of a particularly bright Mars, and that was why they fought so much. They'd met under Mars, he'd proposed under Venus, and I'd been conceived on a night when every star, planet, and light in the sky blazoned for all they were worth. That's why they named me Stella.

We lost Mom on the night of the Torrance Comet. It's called the Torrance Comet because that's where it landed—our little town of Torrance, Indiana, not far from the farm. He and Mom had put me to bed. They went out on the big wraparound porch of the family farmhouse we'd inherited from my daddy's parents.

My dad said that Momma's eyes lit up when she saw the comet rip the sky in half with its golden knife. He said she'd jumped to her feet and whispered, "it's close" before she made a run for it.

My daddy laughed for a moment and finished drinking his beer. He always said he couldn't remember how it tasted, just that even if it had been the best beer in all of God's Kingdom, he'd do anything to undrink it.

By the time he ran after her, she had a full minute head start. Only a minute, but only a minute is all it takes sometimes.

He never saw Momma again.

Daddy looked for an hour. When he called the sheriff, everyone came and helped search. Not just the sheriff, but all Daddy's friends and the pastor and the O'Malleys and the Thorntons and the Wichitas and even those weird Holcombs. That's why Daddy always said I had to be nice to everyone in town. Because when we needed them most, the whole town, no matter how strange or backward I might think them, had gotten up in the middle of the night and looked for Momma.

They never found her. They didn't find her body or any signs of her at all.

All those families did the cooking for Daddy until he learned how to do it on his own.

For about a week, Daddy said, he thought losing Momma would break him. He thought he wouldn't be able to live. Then late one night, he took me outside, and the two of us looked up at the stars. I was too young to remember this.

He said I reached up as high as I could and said my first word — star.

That saved him, he always said. It woke him up and he was alive again. He was my daddy.

I sensed he was hurting all the time, every day, but I also couldn't remember Momma or a time before his grief. It didn't stop him from smiling. It didn't stop him from laughing. It didn't stop him from loving me.

When we sat under the stars together, he would always say he felt like Momma was up there with them, still being a wife and mother. That's why he never dated again. He said Momma would see and wouldn't like it.

By the time I was in my teens, I knew Momma wouldn't have minded, even if she was watching. When you love someone as much as my momma must have loved my daddy, you couldn't begrudge them a little slice of happiness every once in a while.

I felt like everyone in town pitied me, but I didn't pity me. I lived in a big house with a daddy and a great big golden retriever named Mercury, and I didn't really know what I was missing.

~ 2 ~

THE SUMMER I turned sixteen started out the same as all the summers before. I helped Daddy on the farm. I played with Mercury. I read books in trees. I hung out with friends who still preferred soda to beer, and I went about the business of being sixteen and feeling alive.

I was happy.

Bobby O'Malley and I had grabbed burgers at the Shack—mine loaded with everything, Bobby's with nothing but ketchup. Bearing the brown sack in one hand and balancing our shakes in between my arm and my torso, I climbed into Bobby's truck.

Bobby O'Malley, age sixteen, spoke in poetry and lived in blue jeans, muddy boots, and plaid shirts. A spattering of acne crossed a face barely sprouting scruff. Shaggy hair he never cut hung past his ears. The eyes, as they glanced at me in the mirror, were the brown of corn stalks in October.

The truck still smelled of fish guts from a fishing trip last week, which was better than when it smelled like deer hide. In the background, the peculiar mix of mud and sweat always lingered. Just then, though, the smell of burgers and fries filled up the cab as he started the engine and pulled out onto the road.

"Pass me a fry, Small Fry," he said.

"Pass yourself a fry," I said, stuffing at least five into my mouth.

Not taking his eyes off the road, he rummaged in the bag until he found the fries. "Geez, how many have you already eaten?"

"Oh, I plan on eating as many of them as I can get," I said, "especially as I paid for them."

Bobby rolled his eyes and grabbed a wad of fries from the bag as I messed with the dials on the radio.

"Be sure to catch tonight's meteor shower," the radio DJ said. "The show will start around nine. Astronomers are saying it'll be quite the light display."

Bobby glanced over at me with the peculiar mixture of concern and interest that was typical Bobby.

"I'll need to get home in time to be with Daddy," I said.

"Sounds fine. You ever feel a bit…?" His voice trailed off.

"No, I don't, but for Daddy, it's one of those things that's both terrible and beautiful all at once."

Bobby frowned, turning from the road to look at me. "All the best things are." He pulled into a parking lot off the lake. A few trees, a playground, and some picnic tables separated us from the water.

Bobby got out of the car, grabbing his shake, and I followed him out.

A warm wind came off the water. The sun nested in wreaths of oranges and pinks that made a flaming mirror of the lake as we sat down to eat.

"You just can't beat sunsets like this," Bobby said.

"That's Torrance for you."

Bobby smiled. "Best town in the world."

"How's the new poem coming?"

"Would you like to hear it?" he asked through a mouthful of burger.

"Once you've finished chewing."

He swallowed, then jumped up onto the picnic table, nearly knocking over our shakes. A mother and her children glanced over at him from a nearby table.

He cleared his throat. "There was once a girl named Stella, who was a fun friend for a farming fella, but she ain't no Cinderella. She doesn't work in a cella, but she always forgets to bring a candle of citronella."

Bobby took a deep bow.

"Bravo," I clapped. "Though in all fairness, is there anyone under the age of forty-five who ever remembers citronella candles?"

Bobby shrugged as he sat down and finished his

burger. "It was the only thing I could think of to rhyme with Cinderella."

"Very graceful."

"Thank you," he said with a grin. "I knew you'd think so."

"Seriously, though, I want to hear the real poem."

He shook his head. "No, sirree."

"If you're going to be a famous poet, you're going to have to let me read your poems at some point."

"Oh, I will," he said, "when I'm a famous poet. Then you'll be welcome to read along with the masses."

I laughed and finished my own burger. He rested his hand over his cheek and took a long drink of chocolate milkshake. "Look how big Doug Carter's gotten," he said.

I glanced at the kids on the playground. Doug Carter had managed to climb on top of the swing set. He balanced on the top while his mother—and three others—stared blankly; the children watched with wide eyes. His orange hair a mess of dirt, his face a blazing smile, his hands extended on either side of him, he took a bow.

"Thank you, thank you," I heard him say.

And with that, he toppled over into his mother's arms.

The other kids burst into applause. I caught the barest traces of a laugh at the edges of his mother's lips, but that did not stop the steady stream of reprimands as she hauled him away to the car.

"He's kind of insane," Bobby said lightly.

"Kind of?"

Bobby took another long drink of his milkshake. "Meh, I've seen crazier."

I raised an eyebrow, but his attention was on the sunset now. "Penny for your thoughts?" I asked.

"I'm just wondering how a sunset gets to be so…"

"Yeah," I agreed.

As we watched the sunset, a song blared from a passing car. For a moment, the deep bass blended with the passage of the sun, the hum of the wind, and the tang of my strawberry shake.

Wordlessly, we finished our shakes and threw out the trash then got in his truck and started driving.

Bobby and I did a lot of that. We'd take off in his truck and drive. We wouldn't go anywhere in particular. We wouldn't say anything in particular. We wouldn't do anything in particular. We'd just drive. Sometimes, we'd talk family or school or God or the universe or everything. Other times, we'd ride in silence.

That night, the drive took us through town and into the wide sea of cornfields. The rain had been plentiful that year, and the stalks already stretched their proud necks skywards.

"We'll have a good harvest this year," he said.

"If the gods are good." I laughed.

"True. Guess you never know."

The sun's wild corona faded quickly now as Bobby took the twists and turns without slowing down.

"Actually, you'd better take me home," I said. "It's going to start soon."

"Momma O'Malley'll want me home to watch, too."

We were silent for a while after that. It wasn't awkward — not with Bobby.

"I'll miss this place when we're gone," he said.

"We won't be gone long."

Bobby nodded, smiling. "I don't know, Stella Bell, you've got the mysteries of the universe to uncover. Something tells me that could take you pretty far away from Torrance, Indiana."

"Maybe," I said, "or maybe it'll keep me right where I am."

Bobby laughed, throwing back his long hair. He let one hand fall out the window and turned up the song on the radio. The music swirled with the wind through that moment in the car, and I closed my eyes and trailed my own fingers through the sharp breeze.

Then Bobby started bellowing out the words to the song with a thick faux-country croon, and I joined in until the song ended. We laughed all the way up to my own house.

When I got home, I found Daddy on the porch. He grinned as I sat down on the old swing beside him and put my head on his shoulder.

"How's Bobby?" he asked.

"Oh, he's Bobby," I remember saying.

"He tell you he loves you yet?"

I rolled my eyes. "He doesn't love me. Boys and girls can be friends without any of that silly stuff getting in the way."

"Yeah, yeah, so you keep saying. Hey, there's supposed to be a meteor shower tonight."

"I know," I said. "I heard about it on the radio. That's why I came back early."

"Watch it with your old man?"

"I wouldn't watch it with anyone else."

"Not even Bobby O'Malley?" he asked.

I elbowed him in the ribs.

"Okay, okay," he said. "Ahh, there it goes."

I smiled and leaned back, feeling the cool wind ruffle my hair and pretending it was the tail breeze of the falling stars. The meteors fell thick and heavy, burning through the sky with a color and a celerity that was nearly angry.

"Beautiful," my father whispered.

"Magnifico," I agreed.

He squeezed my shoulder, and then he seemed to stiffen. "Hey, old thing, do you see…?" He trailed off, pointing.

"It's going to come down right in the middle of our land," I said.

It was a moment like a scratched record. The song had been playing, and the song had been beautiful, and then it skipped. I could feel the tear run straight through my father's heart—excitement and glory on one side, a projector screen of memories on the other.

My father hated skipping tracks. When a record skipped, he always got up and moved the spindle without a moment's hesitation.

He forced himself just as abruptly and mechanically from the swing. The spindle now back on track, my father stood just a few feet away, his back to me.

Part of me will always be trapped in that moment, seeing my father's old blue jeans, his plaid blue and orange button-up, the glowing light of the stars framing his whole silhouette like a halo. I can still smell him, that mixture of corn and sweat and summer, as he turned his face almost to me so I could see his profile.

"Who wants to chase a comet?" he asked, his voice filled with the hushed reverence of a cathedral.

And before I had the chance to say a word, my daddy leaped off the porch and sprinted into the corn.

I rose slowly, watching him go. The whole night was bathed in golden light as those angry burning balls shredded through the sky. The warmth of my father's arm was still around me, the Shack burger sat heavy in my stomach, and a long drive with Bobby foamed at the back of my thoughts. I leaned against the wood pole of the porch for a moment. I soaked in the night, vowing never to forget that feeling.

Then my dad gave a whooping battle cry of freedom and a meteor light flashed. I shouted out an echo. One breath later, I sprinted after him into the night.

I ran faster than my father. He was fit and strong and still young, but I was sixteen and ran track and cross country during the year. And the light of stars blazed in my veins.

I thought I'd catch him up.

I laughed as I ran. There was something about running beneath a sky like that.

When I reached the corn, I plunged in without pause as I'd done a thousand times before. The wet summer had grown the corn high above my head. The stalks scratched at me, and cobwebs caved in as I ran.

Somewhere ahead, I heard the sound of my father amid the corn.

The great light intensified.

I stopped and looked up. For a split second, I saw the dark core of the meteor before the ground gave a rumble and a shake to welcome it to Earth.

I yelled out, and I heard my father yelling too. I don't know what we yelled. We were swept away on the current of this moment.

I started running again.

I broke through into the first lane when my

father called out my name.

"I found it!" he yelled. "I…"

"Daddy?" I called out, hesitating. Meteors still flashed through the sky. There was still much light to see by. "Daddy?"

My father made no response.

I ran hard.

I got there just in time to see what my father had not seen the first time.

A small crater pockmarked our field. A boulder hunched in its epicenter. My father stood next to the boulder, his hand on the rock.

He was frozen, and a golden light passed all over and around him, spinning a chrysalis around his body even as I stifled a scream.

The last thing the light took was his face. I saw him mouth my name. And then the light covered that, too.

I sprang, bolting down the crater toward him, my hands outstretched. I would pull him free. I would save him. I would…

The light faded to nothing before I reached the rock.

I stood where he'd stood, and I screamed.

I gazed up at those falling stars. They really did look angry.

I don't know how long I stood there under the burning sky, but Bobby O'Malley found me out there.

He appeared through the corn, and with one

glance, he understood. Nothing needed saying. He put an arm around me and guided me back to the O'Malley family farm.

The O'Malley house hulked on a piece of land about half a mile from where I lost my father. Like my own house, it had a wraparound porch, but this house was about twice the size. The O'Malley family owned the largest and most successful of all the farms in Torrance. They also had the most children.

As soon as we broke through the corn, dogs and O'Malleys came running toward us. Bobby had five siblings, three of them younger. Clad in overalls, they sprinted toward us with all the wild joy of the meteors above.

When they saw our faces, though, the stardust burned cold in their veins.

"Where are Momma and Pa?" Bobby asked.

The youngest answered. "Out back."

"Get them now," Bobby said. "Tell 'em it happened again."

The youngest, Martha, was the first to move. Her pigtails flying after her, she tore back across the yard, dogs and siblings yapping at her heels.

"What did you see?" Bobby asked me for the first time as we were left alone.

If I had paused to think, I might not have told him the truth. If I had paused to consider the lunacy of what happened, I might have said nothing at all. If it had been anyone but Bobby, anyone but the person I trusted the second most—no, now it was not the second most, but the most—in all the world, I might have lied.

But I turned to Bobby and whispered. "It was the meteor. It wrapped him up in this cocoon of light and then he was just…"

"Gone?" Bobby asked, his voice a shallow wind.

"Gone."

"We won't tell anyone what you saw," he said. I remember nodding, realizing for the first time how insane my story would sound. "After all, maybe it didn't happen quite the way it looked."

"You don't believe me?" I whispered.

"No, no," Bobby said. "I'm just saying that cornfields in the middle of meteor showers can be deceptive places. Come on."

As we started back up to the house, Bobby's parents burst through the front door. Unlike her six children, Mrs. O'Malley grew low to the earth. Red-faced and dark-haired, she was soft and robust where the other O'Malleys were lean steel.

Mr. O'Malley was tall as the corn but wired for strength. He had a rifle in his hands as he rushed toward us.

"You see anything, Stella Katherine?" he asked me, putting one hand on my shoulder.

"Nothing," I lied. "He was just…"

"Gone?" Mr. O'Malley asked.

"Gone," I agreed.

He planted a kiss on the top of my head. "We'll

find him. I'm heading to your place, and so is Sheriff Donalee and Pastor Bob and the Witchitas, the Thorntons, the Holcombs, everybody. Momma'll take care of you while we look for your daddy."

My head nodded. I couldn't understand why I was not more upset. No tears stung my eyes. No fingers shook. No fear encased my spine. I felt nothing at all.

"It'll be okay." Mr. O'Malley turned and climbed into his truck. From the front door, Bobby's two older brothers came in their turns, both bearing rifles and set faces. Each spared me a quick hug before climbing into the truck.

Last of all, Bobby hugged me tightly. "Don't be afraid," he whispered into my hair.

"I'm not," I said.

And then Bobby, too, climbed into the truck.

Mrs. O'Malley put an arm around me as the engine exploded to life with an eager snarl.

"If he's out there, they'll find him." Mrs. O'Malley was not one for false promises or false hope. She must have remembered that other night better than I did. There must have been promises made that night too. Promises that could only have been broken.

Mrs. O'Malley led me inside, wrapping me in an old patchwork quilt that, once upon a time, I'd helped stitch. She sat me on the couch in their living room and brought me a glass of milk. My fingers traced the stitches my hands had once made, hands that had lost a mother but still had a father. Innocent fingers. Happy fingers.

Mrs. O'Malley split her time between me, the telephone, and the kitchen. Martha crawled up next to me and lay her head on my lap. At some point in the night, the other siblings appeared with Mercury. He nuzzled into my side and watched.

All that night, the room bustled with people. They came, and they went. When they came, they watched me. And when they went, they whispered about me in voices too loud for their fear not to travel.

But there was nothing to be afraid of. The worst had already happened.

One by one, the O'Malley siblings dropped off to sleep.

"I've made you up a bed," Mrs. O'Malley told me at one point.

"Please," I found myself saying. "I'd rather just stay here."

"But, honey, you need your sleep," she said. "I promise I'll wake you up just as soon as we hear something."

I shook my head. "I won't be able to sleep. It's better this way."

Mrs. O'Malley looked at me with eyes older than her years. Eyes that might have remembered my father saying something similar on a night much like this one. "All right, sweetheart," she said.

Mrs. O'Malley carried her children to their beds one by one, all but Martha who woke when she tried to move her.

"I won't leave her," Martha said in a matter of fact tone.

Mrs. O'Malley knew Martha too well to argue, so she let Martha be.

As soon as Mrs. O'Malley left, Martha dropped right back to sleep.

Mercury never slept though, and neither did I. All through the night, his eyes remained wide and staring, watching the front door. Waiting.

I wondered if he knew there was nothing to wait for.

~ 3 ~

I WATCHED the first golden sparks of morning fall on the wood floor of the O'Malley family living room. The light fell on Mercury's fur and made it glow like molten gold. I sank my fingers into that gold.

In the kitchen, I could hear low voices. Mrs. O'Malley, Mrs. Wichita, and the sheriff's wife, Mrs. Donalee, were all in there. They spoke low, and the sizzle of bacon and the fizz of eggs masked the words. I didn't need to hear the words, though, to know what they were saying.

A few minutes later, a pair of eyes appeared at the edge of the doorway, and then I heard the scampering of a child's feet.

"She's awake!" I heard one of the O'Malley siblings say.

After that, Mrs. O'Malley came bustling in. "Wake up, Martha."

Martha moaned but sat up, wiping at her face with the sleeve of her pajamas.

"Stella, dear, won't you... what's wrong? Did I wake you? Karen said you were awake."

The sound of my own name struck me like a slap.

"No, no," I said, "I... you just startled me, that's all. I was awake."

Mrs. O'Malley looked at me with pity in those big brown eyes. "Well, come on," she said. "We've got breakfast made, and you need to eat. No point going hungry. There never is."

The thought of food—its thick smell already filling up the whole of the O'Malley downstairs—sickened me, but I let myself be pulled up from the sofa and guided along the hall in the direction of the kitchen.

The O'Malley halls were more pictures than walls. Snapshots, Polaroids, and photographs crowded all the available space. History smiled from the O'Malley family smiles in a hundred pictures of lost days.

I'd always loved those pictures. The story of the whole town could be found in those frames. I could find my mother there.

I paused before that picture, the one two up and three to the right from the coffee table where nestled the carcass of the old landline, just before the door to a closet. My momma stood with an arm around my father and an arm around Mrs. O'Malley. My daddy held me in his arms. My parents looked so young. In the picture, my mother's wild hair strained to break free from the band holding it back, and her eyes... her eyes were star bright. All their eyes were star bright, even mine. I wondered how

Daddy had done it. I looked into Daddy's eyes in the photograph. They'd never changed. Maybe a little sadder, but they'd never gone out. I don't know how he'd managed that. I felt like every star in all the universe of universes had gone out for me.

In the photograph, Mrs. O'Malley looked just exactly the same—red-faced, kind, and warm.

In this moment, Mrs. O'Malley paused. Her eyes traveled from mine to the photograph.

"Not a day goes by when I don't miss her," she said softly, wrapping an arm around my shoulder. "Your momma was like a sister to me. Everyone always loved your mother. She was always just so free. Like you, Stella."

I flinched at the name, and Mrs. O'Malley took a step back from me. Her eyes were beginning to put it together. "Come along, sweetheart. The food won't help, I know, but you've got to eat until time does."

Letting out a breath, I let her lead me. Mercury padded along at my heels, brushing my leg every few minutes, as if to remind me he was there.

When we reached the kitchen, I braced myself for the faces I would see, for the voices, for the arms, for the words that could come with an onslaught of kindness and charity. Words and eyes and arms so warm that in this moment, I knew they would burn.

But as I stepped into the kitchen and saw the women gathered there, the women who I knew had been out all night roaming through tree and field with rifles, I remembered. The women of Torrance understood loss.

In a swirl of activity and the wind of quiet

voices, I found myself sitting at the kitchen table with a plate of eggs. By the glass door, Mercury ate from an old silver bowl. And the women around me talked of the harvest and their children.

"Did you hear what Doug Carter did last night?" Mrs. Wichita asked.

"I heard no such thing," Mrs. Donalee said.

"I heard it from his mother," Mrs. Holcomb chimed in. "That boy will be the death of her."

"What on earth did he do?" Mrs. O'Malley asked.

"I heard you were there, Stella Katherine, when it happened?" Again, I flinched under the palm of my name.

"I... yes," I said. "At the park, you mean?"

"Yes, yes." Mrs. Holcomb busied herself with something in the oven.

"Oh no," Mrs. O'Malley said, "what has the child done now? Wasn't it just last week that he set fire to his daddy's shed playing around with matches?"

"And the week before that, he got himself stuck up on the roof of the old church," Mrs. Holcomb said. "Patty thought the place was haunted. She kept hearing that little devil child on the roof while she was practicing her organ for Sunday and thinking there were ghosts in the belfries."

"Until she heard the ghost singing a rather recent and hideous pop song," Mrs. Donalee laughed. The story was well known and well rehearsed by now.

"And she went out and found wild Doug Carter singing at the top of his lungs with half the roof's shingles on the ground," said Mrs. Holcomb.

"It took the fire department two hours to get him off because he kept running away from poor Mitch," Mrs. O'Malley added.

The women all laughed, and somehow, remarkably, I found myself laughing, too.

"So what's he done now?" Mrs. Donalee asked.

"Well, nothing so wild in comparison," said Mrs. Holcomb.

"Why don't you tell it, Stella Katherine, as you were there?" Mrs. Wichita asked, patting my hand.

"Oh, he got on top of the swingset," I explained. "And then he kind of bowed and fell off. But Mrs. Carter managed to catch him."

Mrs. O'Malley shook her head with a laugh. "Well, the top of a swingset is no church roof, but you can break your neck either way."

"That's God's truth," said Mrs. Wichita.

"None of her others were ever like that," Mrs. Donalee chimed in.

"Darren and Dina and Derek are all just as peaceful and as quiet as pigs wrapped in a blanket," said Mrs. Wichita.

"There's always the one," remarked Mrs. Holcomb darkly.

"Ain't that the truth," Mrs. O'Malley agreed.

"And here was me thinking all mine turned out so wonderfully. I was actually wanting Wichita Jr. to get out of the house more."

"Oh no, what's Wichita Jr. got himself up to?" Mrs. Donalee asked.

Mrs. Holcomb glowered. "I don't know. Years, I couldn't get him to put down his video games and go out. Now, he's always disappearing. I don't know what that boy is up to."

Just then, the glass door of the kitchen slid open and Bobby O'Malley trooped inside.

Bobby was encrusted with a layer of dried, cracking mud from the bottoms of his boots to the caps of his blue jean-clad knees. He heaved a yawn as he entered. A long streak of mud ran from his ear across his cheek.

All the women hushed as he slid the door closed behind him.

"Well?" Mrs. O'Malley asked.

He turned to gaze at the room. In that expression, I'd have found my answers, if I'd needed them, without a single word exchanged. The eyes were red. The mud brown of them was flat and lightless.

"Nothing," he said. "But no one's giving up. They sent me back to help you all load up breakfast and check on Stella Bell." He saw me wince, and his eyes searched my face for answers.

"Did they get done with the Thompson land?" asked Mrs. Holcomb.

"Yes, ma'am," Bobby answered as his mother set a plate of eggs, bacon, and toast before him.

"And the woods out by 37?"

"Yes'm," Bobby answered through a mouthful of food. As Bobby ate, the women busied themselves loading up all the food they'd prepared for the searchers. Bobby watched me closely as he finished off his food. He did it from his periphery, true, but I could tell his eyes never left me.

When he'd eaten, he leaned forward. "Stella Bell," he began, leaning across the table.

Again, I flinched.

"What is it?" he asked.

Mrs. O'Malley swatted Bobby's ear and hissed. "What does her name mean, Mr. High IQ?"

"Oh," he said.

"I'm all right," I said, even though technically no one had asked. But at the sound of those words coming out of my mouth, the strain became too much. The lock burst.

I did what I prided myself on never doing. I let out a sob.

In the next moment, I felt Mercury's nose nudging my knees, Bobby's long, gangly arms around me, Mrs. O'Malley's on top of those, Mrs. Donalee's on top of those, and so on and so forth. And I let myself cry.

In retrospect, I'm glad I did. I haven't cried again in all these years since.

That moment went on for a miniature infinity. I couldn't say if it lasted thirty seconds or thirty minutes. The warm enclosure of those arms has never really left me. But it ended. Bobby and the women took the food and left.

Mrs. O'Malley led me up to the guest bed, and it was only then, with full sunlight pouring through sheer white curtains, that I fell asleep.

~ 4 ~

I WOKE to the transformation of the golden light into the oranges and pinks of sunset. For a moment, I stared out the window at the purple-hued sky. The bed was warm and soft. At the end of the bed, Mercury stood a silent sentry as he must have all day. Somewhere in the house, I could hear feet and voices and movement. From the barely open window, I heard the sound of other voices, many voices.

And I remembered why I was here.

The walls of the guest room were plain and bare. A wooden dresser sat in one corner near a small walk-in closet. The room had its own bathroom.

I closed my eyes and put it off. I put off rising. I put off going downstairs. I put off listening to the reports of what they hadn't found. I put off making plans for what to do in the After. I supposed it was the After that I wanted to put off. After Daddy. The rest of my life would be After Daddy now. There was no putting it off. Not really. I had been living in it from the moment I saw him firework into golden sparks.

I sat up and Mercury sprang up onto the bed. I wrapped my arms around his warm body.

Decisions needed making. Lies needed telling. Compromises with myself needed forging. And down below, I knew it was all waiting. A whole life. The rest of my life.

I let Mercury go. I showered. I dried my hair. I looked in the mirror. And I went downstairs to face it.

Downstairs, I found much of the town.

The town had looked as hard for my father as they had for my mother all those years ago. Everyone from the sheriff to the pastor to the O'Malleys and the Wichitas and the Thorntons and the Holcombs searched.

And now, all those families stood in the living room of the O'Malley house. Their eyes tired, and their clothes dirty.

When I entered the room, a hush fell.

Sheriff Donalee emerged from the faces. The sheriff was a man of medium height and medium build, stomach strained at the waist of his uniform. His eyes were hard and deep. His wife rested her hand on his back.

I felt Mrs. O'Malley's arm around my shoulder.

"Stella, sweetheart," Sheriff Donalee began. I forced aside the flinch at the word. I knew what he would say. I wondered how many times the sheriff of a small town like Torrance had to have these conversations. I thought it must be more than I could guess. "We couldn't find your daddy. We looked everywhere, but we couldn't find hide nor hair of him. I think... I think that it's like what happened to your ma. I think he's just..."

"Gone," I said for him.

"Gone," he confirmed.

"Thank you for searching." I turned to look at the room, to look at Holcombs and Wichitas and O'Malleys and Donalees, at Carters and the rest. "Thank you all for searching for my daddy just like you did for my... for my momma. I want you to know that I... I can't tell you how much I..." I took a deep breath and steadied myself. I found Bobby in the crowd, and I held onto his eyes. "I want you to know that I am so incredibly grateful to each and every one of you for what you've done for my family."

"It's what neighbors do, sweetheart," Mrs. Donalee said, threading her arm around her husband's.

"And you are the very best of neighbors," I said.

After that, they slowly made their way from the living room and from the O'Malley house. Headlights flared to life outside, casting bright shadows on the living room walls as, family by family, they left.

When they were gone, I stood in the living room with the O'Malley family. "And I... I wanted to thank you most of all," I said. "I don't know what I..."

"Stop all that," Mrs. O'Malley said.

"You're family, Ste—" Bobby bit off the end of my name.

"And you're going to stay with us now," Mrs.

O'Malley said gently, "if that's all right with you. We'd like to have you here with us, and we'd like to take care of you. Does that... does that sound fine?"

"Can Mercury come, too?" I asked.

"We wouldn't have you here without him."

I gazed from strawberry-faced Mrs. O'Malley to the tall cornstalk of Mr. O'Malley to Martha's flint eyes and Bobby's muddy smile.

"That sounds wonderful," I said.

"Good," Mr. O'Malley said, betraying more emotion in the one word than I'd ever heard from him.

"Now, we should just run over to your house, pick up some of your things, so you have a proper change of clothes and everything," said Mrs. O'Malley.

I walked with Mrs. O'Malley onto the porch. For the first time since last night, I felt the wind coming off the corn.

As I stepped out from under the roof of the porch, I froze. The sky was ablaze.

I couldn't move.

Mrs. O'Malley tracked my stare. "Why don't you go back inside, dear? I'll just nip over, pick up your things, and be right back."

At first, I could make no response. Then I forced my head to nod.

Bobby came and led me back up the steps.

From the window of the living room, I watched Mrs. O'Malley drive away. I stepped away from the window as my eyes went upwards and turned my back.

That night, I closed and locked the window. I

drew the thick blinds down, turned on every light in the room, and I waited for the sun to rise.

At about midnight, a gentle knock came at the door.

"Come in," I said.

The door opened, and Bobby stepped inside. "I saw the light. Can't sleep?"

I shook my head. Bobby crossed the room and sat down at the end of my bed, scratching behind Mercury's sleepy ears.

"How are you doing?" he asked.

I shrugged. "About how one might expect."

There was a moment in which only the sound of crickets and Mercury's breathing could be heard. "So what do you think it was?" he asked at last.

"I don't know."

"You think whatever it was that got your daddy is the same thing that got your momma?"

"I think that's a safe assumption."

"You think it was the meteors?"

"I saw what I saw."

Bobby nodded, his hands moving on from Mercury's ears to his back. "Maybe the Ancient Greeks had it right," he murmured.

"What do you mean?"

"Maybe all the stars really are gods and goddesses," he whispered, his eyes on the thick curtains hiding us from the sky. The curtains were made from a heavy white fabric embroidered with splotches of blue and fuchsia flowers.

"You think the thing that killed my parents was a god?" I asked, my voice laden with yet another emotion too complicated for me to pin down.

"The gods and goddesses weren't all good," Bobby said. "They were just people, each with their own caprices, none to be truly trusted, all of them manipulating our lives in ways both subtle and obvious."

"You sound like a textbook." I tried to laugh.

"Well," he shrugged, "I may have been doing some research before I came in here."

"But what would gods and goddesses want with my parents?"

Bobby shrugged again. "Who can understand the will of the gods? But sometimes, the gods got angry. Sometimes, they got jealous of humans they felt were threats to themselves. Sometimes, they fell in love, and half the time, when they fell in love, it just ended terribly for the humans involved. Maybe some god fell in love with your mother or was jealous or…"

"But why both of them? Why take both of them?" I asked.

"Maybe the gods need a sacrifice."

The word hung suspended and glittering in the air until I waved it away.

"There are other explanations," I said.

"Oh yeah? Reasonable, scientific explanations, you mean?"

"Exactly, Mr. Poet. Just because something isn't known by science, doesn't mean it can't be scientifically explained."

"That's true," Bobby agreed. "You always did want to unravel the secrets of the universe."

"And I still do," I said, realizing only then that the words were still true. The realization constituted a shred of something solid to stand on. It gave me not only continuity between Before and After, but also formed the wispy, smoke outline of a possible future.

"Good, I'm glad." Bobby smiled. "Hey, you wanna play cards?"

"Yes." I nodded. "I would very much like to play cards."

Bobby stayed up with me all night. We played round after round, first of war and then of go fish and then poker. On and on and on, until the first slivers of sunlight snuck past those thick curtains, and I felt almost safe once again. Bobby slipped out. I slipped into sleep.

~ 5 ~

THE NEXT DAY was the first of many days with the O'Malley family. The work of farms does not stop for personal tragedy, and I was grateful for that. It meant there was work to be done and normalcy to be partaken in. And so I planned to partake.

That first morning, I changed into clothes suitable for working on a farm. Mercury padding after me, I went down to the kitchen. The O'Malley family would have started work hours before. Mrs. O'Malley had left me breakfast. Although I did not want to eat it, I did.

While the O'Malley family had much to do on their own much larger farm, there was much to be done on my daddy's. I couldn't let his disappearance destroy what he'd spent his life on, what his parents and their parents and their parents had spent their lives on.

The shortest path from O'Malley land to mine

was through the fields. Bobby and I carved that path and memorized it as children. I took it again now.

The morning sun blanketed the fields with its golden lights. The morning was cool, but I could feel the promise of heat in the air. You always could feel it out in the fields. The cornstalks and cobwebs reached out for me as I passed, Mercury running up ahead of me.

There was a point where the O'Malley land ended and the Callahan land began, an invisible line in the corn you could only feel but never see. Callahan land knew my feet. Callahan land was my birthright.

I didn't think I'd have anything to fear from the soil of my family, but as I crossed that invisible line, a wrongness started from the soles of my boots up to the ends of my hair. The Callahan land. It was mine now. I didn't want it to be mine now. It was too soon.

A cloud passed before the sun, and a great shadow fell across the fields.

"I'm being silly," I said. Up ahead, Mercury barked. In his bark, there was no fear. There was only summertime and doghood.

I forced my feet onward. There was work to be done.

There was work to be done. I couldn't let my father down.

I tried to force my feet onward.

But my feet abandoned the path. My feet took

me away from the well-worn passage between O'Malley country and my own to the one place they shouldn't go.

With a final long scratch of corn stalk across my face, I stepped out into the small crater where Daddy met the meteor.

That hunk of rock stared up at me. It could have been any rock. There was nothing about its appearance to suggest it was Heaven born.

My feet moved me across the gutted corn down to the boulder. I placed a hand against the rough surface. It felt like any rock. There was nothing in its touch that warned of heavens or of danger, of the predator that stole my father.

I let my hand fall.

A shudder tore through my back, and my knees dug into the earth. This wasn't sobbing. This wasn't crying. This was something else entirely. I couldn't breathe. My heart hammered so hard, I thought it would shatter my skeleton in its race to escape whatever terror seized it. I gasped for breath, but no breath would come. I tried to cry for help, but I could make no sound. My mind became a meteor then—entering the atmosphere, shattering into a thousand broken, blazing pieces of burning star, of killer.

This time of falling was yet another in a long string of infinite moments I encountered in the days surrounding my father's disappearances. Time's grip on me seemed fragile, as if it held me with slick fingers.

Eventually, time resumed. Strong arms found me, lifted me, and bore me away. I caught my first real breath the moment I passed back from Callahan land onto O'Malley land.

Bobby set me down at the base of a tree we used to climb. An inch from where my head rested, there was a carving of a star. I'd done it a decade ago. Up among the higher branches, hidden by thick leaves, we'd carved our initials and a promise: BO + SC FOREVER. We carved it at seven years old. We hid it because it wasn't romance we were symbolizing; it was the loyalty of fellow knights. Of best friends. All too often, people misunderstood. Like my father always did. They saw romance where there was something just as good, or even better—friendship. The fact that Bobby's initials could also be read as Body Odor did not enter our thoughts until much, much later.

Now, I gazed at the star I'd carved into the bark.

"St... Katie, are you okay?" Bobby asked.

"Yes... Yes, I'm fine. Thank you. I needed to get some things done on the farm."

"We're doing all of that. It's no trouble."

I opened my eyes the rest of the way and sat up. "No, no, my daddy never... he…"

"Your daddy would want the Callahan land taken care of. And your daddy understood a neighbor's job is to pitch in. Remember when my whole family came down with mono? And you and your daddy helped for months?"

I couldn't forget that. The work had been nightmarish. I'd thought it would never end. "Yes. Believe it or not, I remember that quite vividly."

Bobby smiled lightly. "Well, now, it's our turn."

"But, Bobby, I don't know... I don't know if I can ever go back." The words were out of my lips before I had time to think about them.

"Ever is a large word for four letters. But if you can't go back, you can always help on our farm, and we'll do yours. We help each other."

"We help each other," I echoed, laying my head against the bark. I don't think my daddy would have minded that. I didn't mind that.

"You have lunch?" Bobby asked.

"Lunch?"

"Yeah, it's almost noon. Come on up to the house with me and eat. Then, if you want, we'll put you to work."

He stood up and offered me his hand. I managed to smile up at his face, which, acne or not, was now my favorite face.

He helped me up and then grinned. "Race ya!" And then he was off, tearing through the corn.

"What! I wasn't ready!" I called after him. For a moment, I hesitated, the sick feeling of the land still gnawing the base of my stomach, but I pushed the feeling aside. I tore off after him and managed to beat him to the house, even with his head start. I was not about to let grief tarnish my undefeated record in races with Bobby O'Malley.

~ 6 ~

OVER THE REST of the summer, I threw myself into the farm. I worked until I was too tired not to sleep at night. I worked until I was too tired to feel my grief except in the very marrow of my bones.

There were interruptions, of course.

One interruption was the funeral.

The funeral took place at Torrance Baptist Church. It was the church where my parents were married, where I was baptized.

There were only three churches in Torrance: the Baptist church, the Catholic church, and the non-denominational upstart church that people didn't like to talk about much. I'd gone every Sunday to the Baptist church all my life. Not a day went by in Torrance without passing by the outside of the church with its white walls and its steeple, which was the tallest point in town. There was a town ordinance that decreed no building should ever be taller than the steeple of the church because no building should ever aspire to place itself above God.

The inside of the church was as familiar and as well-trod a part of my memory as any other place in Torrance. I'd fidgeted my way into young adulthood in these pews, until I could sit through a service with poise and attention. I'd sung in the children's choir on the stage. Pastor Bob had held my nose and dunked me beneath the clear water in the baptistry and declared me saved. I'd attended Sunday School lessons in the classrooms with their peeling stickers of Bible figures. I'd made my stage debut here as a shepherd before working my way up to angel. At Easter, I always begged to play Roman centurions, but those parts always went to Bobby or one of the other boys.

The stained glass windows with their shepherds and stars peopled my childhood daydreams. In my daydreams, the shepherds wore superhero tights beneath their clothes as they followed that star.

The day of the funeral, though, the familiar church was a stranger. Or I was. The pews were the same. The brown halls and the old musty smell was the same. The peeling Bible figure stickers on classroom walls were the same. The old hymnals in the backs of the pews were the same. But when I looked up and saw that star the shepherds followed, no fear of blasphemy could chill the shudder tickling up my spine.

Was that star alive, too? Maybe it was. Maybe there were good stars and bad.

Pastor Bob did the service. I couldn't tell you what Pastor Bob said. It involved Heaven and home and hope and another world. I think what he said was good. I think people heard it, and it helped. Maybe it even helped me, the same way that a nightlight helped a child, or the way a little whistle on the way past a graveyard helped a passerby.

I didn't really know, and I don't really remember.

Everyone was very kind. I remember that much. I remember everyone was kind and soft, and there was food everywhere for weeks on end. Food I had to eat even though I wasn't hungry. Food that tasted like mud going down, even when I knew the food was good.

I remember it was at the wake that I did it. I said it to Pastor Bob the first time. He was the first, and he came up to me as I stood beside an empty casket, a wreath, and poster-boards overflowing with old photographs someone, not me, had put together.

"Stella, I'm so sorry for your loss," he said.

"Thanks," I said. "Call me Katie."

I remember shocking even myself when I said it, and then I remember not having the energy to feel the shock. And I remember the desperation with which I'd told everyone who spoke to me that day to call me Katie. I said those words over and over again. Looking back, I can't imagine doing something like that. I can't imagine having the gall to ask people to call me something other than the name I'd been called all my life.

But every time I heard my name, I felt a slap across the face of my soul. It was an act of desperate self-defense, of survival.

When I'd said it that first time, Pastor Bob didn't blink. He didn't miss a beat. "Ah, I can understand why. Well, Katie, I'm very sorry for your loss. And I hope that one day, you'll be able to bear the name again."

"Thank you," I'd said.

The conversation replayed itself, and by the end of the day, the girl stepping out of her black funeral dress, was Katie, not Stella. And Katie, for some reason, could do what Stella could not.

Yet there were a lot of things I still couldn't do after that night, as Stella or as Katie. Everyone understood, of course. Everyone was very kind. And I remembered what my daddy always said about our town, about how they were there for us when Momma disappeared. Well, they were there for me then. And they didn't say a word when I stopped going out after dark. When I asked people to call me by the name without the connection to the cosmos. When I turned over the running of my own farm to the O'Malleys and couldn't bear to set foot on my own property.

When I started to rewrite so much of what I was.

But the summer went on without the nights, and I kept going. Katie kept going.

Towards the end of that first summer, we drew up a contract. The O'Malley family would help me run it for the next six years, keeping everything going, sharing the profits. At the end of six years, we would talk. That would give me time to finish high school, to start college, and to finish college. Six years.

~ 7 ~

AFTER GRADUATION, most of the kids in our town either went to the local community college or simply went on working their family farms without the inconvenience of higher education. When I was small, my plan had always been to study Astronomy at the closest school that would have me.

Those next two years until graduation were hard. I got through thanks to the kindness of Torrance. I got through and graduated with the grades to get me a scholarship to a school in a city far away. A city where the lights and the smoke would hide me from the sky.

On a late August afternoon, with the sun still safely in its place, Bobby and I drove in his truck through town one last time. I'd told no one this, but I did not plan on coming back. I think we both knew it. He drove those streets, passing every landmark and every memory like we were saying goodbye.

Bobby talked, and I half-listened. "...said the poetry class was really good. I'm pretty nervous, though, to show people."

"You never have shown me any of your poems," I said.

Bobby laughed, but there was a note of strain in that laugh. The thought of sharing his poetry really, truly made him nervous, especially with the prospect of sharing his words becoming increasingly real.

"What about you? Are you nervous to leave?" he asked.

I looked past Bobby out the window. The lake shimmered with reflected light. You could almost think the lake was light. "No... Nervous isn't the right word."

"What is the right word?" he asked.

"I don't know. I... I love Torrance. It has to be one of the best places in the world, but..."

"But it's time." Bobby injected the statement with as much false enthusiasm as he could muster. The attempt fell flat.

"I'll miss you."

"I'll miss you, too, Katie." The way he said my name never rolled off the tongue. I could always hear that moment of hesitation, even two years later.

"So what do you think? Burgers at the Shack? A sunset picnic at the lake?"

I shook my head. "Yes to the burgers. No to the

sunset."

"Fine by me." He pulled into the Shack.

As always, the door of the Shack hung open as families spilled in and out. In front of the Shack, kids ran around, over, and underneath the wooden benches and tables while parents talked to each other and to other parents, all with one eye or both on the mad melee of small children.

I waved as I spotted Mrs. Holcomb across the lot.

Inside, the line to the counter was long, the linoleum floor slick with grease, and the smell of sizzling burgers hummed through the air. Boisterous voices and music over loudspeakers made it difficult to hear.

Bobby and I got in line behind Mrs. Carter.

"Hi, Mrs. Carter," I said.

Mrs. Carter turned and smiled. Beside her, Dina Carter, about to start her sophomore year of high school, echoed her mother's smile. Dina and her mother looked much alike. They had the same wild shock of red hair, but Mrs. Carter appeared exhausted in a way I hope Dina never experienced.

"I drove here," Dina announced.

"Oh my gosh, have you already got your license?" I asked.

"Just her learner's." Mrs. Carter gave us a light smile.

"I'm a fantastic driver," Dina said.

"Actually, she isn't bad," Mrs. Carter said when we looked to her for confirmation.

"How are the boys?" I asked.

"Oh, Derek went back to college Tuesday and Darren's working tonight." She pointed behind the counter, where I could just make out a sweaty redhead leaning over a frier. "And as for Doug…" She let out a deep breath. "He's God knows where."

"Oh, he's just outside." Bobby left out the part where Doug, now all of twelve, was smoking. The sight of Doug smoking around town was common enough these days, and no one wanted to remind his mother of it.

She sighed, hearing the unspoken words. "It's enough to make me want to take up the habit." She shook her head.

"He'll grow out of it," Dina insisted to her mother. Everyone present, including Dina, knew it was a lie.

I'd spent too much of the last two years with Mrs. O'Malley to be tempted to give her a false promise of such growth. Mrs. Carter shook her head. "He will or he won't. He's a human being with God-given free will. It's up to him. Oh, here we go. Dina, you order first. It was so nice seeing you both. Good luck at college, St-Katie."

"Thanks," I said.

After they'd placed their order, they moved off to a corner table to wait. We ordered our own food: my burger with everything, Bobby's with only ketchup, two large orders of fries, one chocolate shake, and one strawberry shake.

When the order came, we waved a goodbye to the Carter family. Doug's cigarette had disappeared. He almost looked like a normal twelve-year-old as we left, stuffing what appeared to be his entire burger into his mouth at once.

"We've got a while before sunset," Bobby said as we climbed into his truck. "Fancy a pre-sunset picnic?"

"As long as it's pre-sunset."

Bobby drove us to the lake, and we sat down at the usual table. Kids played on the swings. A rather furtive young couple nestled out by the water.

"Who do you think that is?" I nodded towards the couple.

"The girl is Edna Holcomb. I can't really tell about the boy from here. They look in love."

"Yeah," I agreed, taking a large bite out of my burger.

We ate in silence, our thoughts filled with a thousand other picnics. The quiet filled with all the words we had for each other, emotions we felt for each other, things people just didn't say out loud. Movies always say you should tell people how you feel, but Bobby and I didn't need to do any telling. There are other ways to share besides words. The silence, the warm wind, the children laughing, the murmur of the waves on the shore, even the sounds of chewing said everything that needed saying.

Bobby got us back well ahead of the sunset. Just as I'd asked.

That last night, I stayed up later than normal. I sat out on the porch and listened to the crickets. I watched the kids run with the dogs, both the O'Malley dogs and Mercury. I listened to the soft conversation of the older O'Malleys.

I didn't say much myself. I didn't like being outside at night, even with the O'Malleys close and a porch roof over my head.

I forced myself to look at the sky only once. As always in that part of the world, the sky blazed with all its glory.

And one glance was enough to tighten my throat and hasten my pulse.

I went to bed after that and waited for the sun to rise on the first day of the rest of my life. I held tight to Mercury for one last night.

The next day, I left Torrance. At the time, I thought it was for good.

I should have known better.

~ 8 ~

IN THE CITY, I could go out at night because neon lights and pollution hid the stars. In the City, I didn't have to be afraid of crossing invisible lines into panic attacks. In the City, when I said my name was Katie, no one questioned me or got it wrong. In the City, no one knew I had a bad history with meteors.

In the City, I found something like freedom, my first taste of it in a very long time.

I still studied Astronomy, as I always planned. To study Astronomy in the City meant studying something existing only in theory. From the safety of the City, I could look down at photographs and gaze through telescopes and know none of it was real here. Such things were only real in other places. In places like Torrance.

I studied Astronomy with the understanding that what I sought was not what the other Astronomy students sought. They came with their eyes full of stars and equations, with dreams of NASA. Some dreamed of spaceships and some just liked telescopes. No one else came with war in their hearts. No one else came looking for what I did.

I came for answers.

My expectations were not unrealistic. I did not expect to come to college, ask my professors about meteor monsters, and be given all the truths I could ask for. I expected to go to college, keep my mouth shut, and sift through the river of information for a single kernel that might reflect just a little light from some truth as yet uncaught by science.

As it turned out, even this was unrealistic. While I enjoyed my program and learned much, I learned nothing that cast any light on the past.

I told no one about my real reason for studying Astronomy. I studied. I went to class. I made friends. I dated. I went to concerts. I watched movies. I read books. For four years, I was almost normal.

In the secret places, though, when I was alone, I started researching, compiling, connecting, shifting, sorting. Disappearances under cosmic events dated back hundreds of years. Everything from meteor showers to auroral lights to eclipses. The stories were out there. They just needed connecting.

I told no one, not even Bobby, about my research. I knew what they would think. So I kept my secrets from everyone. From Torrance and from the new city.

Answers, as it turned out, were few.

And an alternative answer began to grow. An answer I'd considered often over the years, but didn't begin to overtake all other explanations until my third year away from Torrance.

I had gone to see a therapist.

According to Dr. Voorhies, the brain is the source of all mystery. The right combination of fear and love can induce the most hideous, glorious, and convincing of hallucinatory realities. That night under the falling stars, Dr. Voorhies told me, provided the perfect canvas upon which the brain could wreak its terrible masterpiece.

I argued with the good doctor. I told her it never happened before and never since. I questioned if what I saw wasn't what happened, then what did?"

Her answer was so dull and so unsatisfying it could only be the truth. "The reality is you will probably never know what happened to either of your parents," she told me. "Their disappearances could have everything to do with each other or nothing to do with each other. The only thing we really know for sure is that they are both gone. And no amount of magical meteor monsters can bring them back or settle your longing for them. Those monsters leave you only with a false name, an inability to enjoy the stars, and a terror of your own past. You need to accept the most terrifying reality of all. You will not ever know the truth. But that doesn't mean you can't live a perfectly happy life."

After Dr. Voorhies delivered that little nugget of

wisdom, I canceled all my appointments with her, quit taking the medication, and resolved never to see another therapist as long as I lived. The words stayed with me, though, as much as I wished to banish them into nonexistence. Just like I couldn't simply wish away what I'd seen in those cornfields the night of Daddy's disappearance, I couldn't simply wish away what she'd said.

The words floated slowly downward through mind and memory and soul and settled somewhere at the bottom of me. And slowly, I began to think maybe, after all this time, the good doctor was right.

Of course, there were no meteor monsters. Of course, there was no scientific explanation for something that hadn't really happened. Of course, my big file full of clippings and Internet articles about disappearances and mysteries under cosmic phenomena were only the half-crazed rantings of people like me. Sad people full of love and fear who had lost what the mind could not stand to lose.

I never went back to Dr. Voorhies, but she might like to know that I almost came to believe her. But only ever almost.

Dr. Voorhies had told me one other thing that day.

"You need to go back," she said. "You need to go back to your parents' house, and you need to see those people that you clearly love. And you need to let them love you. And you need to call yourself by your name. The one we all know is really yours."

I thought she might be on to something there. Even if she was wrong about the hallucinations. She did have a point when it came to my name.

~ 9 ~

THE SUMMER after I graduated from college, I went home. The six years of my contract with the O'Malleys were up.

I had avoided Torrance from the moment I left. But with school done and grad school still on the horizon, the O'Malley family wanted me back. Our contract was up for negotiation. I told them I wanted them to have everything. They told me they wanted me to stand on the land, to sleep in my old bedroom, drive the old roads, look up at the old stars before I made up my mind. They said they wouldn't sign unless I did.

I was grateful. It gave me an excuse to go home. I think I'd been looking for one. I wanted to face my fear. Out in a place where the night really held dangers, where there was such a thing as sky and stars.

In the middle of June, I flew home.

Bobby was supposed to pick me up from the airport. I was nervous—nervous I wouldn't recognize him after four years away and nervous we wouldn't have anything to say to each other. Then I was nervous about seeing the people of Torrance. What would they think of this person on whom they had lavished so much love, who had deserted the first chance she got?

I tried to make the walk from the plane to the wide vestibule of glass where I'd find Bobby last. I avoided the moving walkways. Dragging my suitcase behind me, I walked slowly. The message on my phone told me Bobby was waiting.

I saw him standing at the end of the little tunnel. He'd cut his long hair short. It was darker now, and his jaw stronger. He appeared taller and wider than I remembered. But his eyes. His eyes, even from this distance, were the same muddy river eyes I'd always known. I shouldn't have feared forgetting his face.

I ran the rest of the way.

I threw myself on him, and we hugged. I felt my arms trying to reclaim all the hugs I'd stolen from myself and from him in one big hug. His arms were strong and tight around me.

"Ka-" he started.

"Stella. You can call me Stella." I stepped out of the hug and smiled.

"I'm glad you're here," he smiled back.

"Me too."

"Momma and Pa can't wait to see you."

I smiled. "I can't wait to see them, too."

As we walked to his truck, we fell into the old patterns. Words came easily, and the silence wasn't scary. He told me about his own time in college, his degree in Poetry. "I'm going to be the Great Farmer Poet."

"You'll be a great one," I said as I got into the truck. It was the same as I remembered with its cracking silver paint and its thin webwork veneer of rust. Inside, the same old smell of ancient mud and sweat still clung just like always. As the buckle clicked on the third try, I thought this moment could have been years ago. Nothing had changed.

But as I looked up from the buckle to Bobby as he started the car, I understood he had changed. And so had I. And so had we. And nothing could be done about it. Although, I thought maybe that wasn't such a bad thing.

"How is everyone at home?" I asked.

"Same old, same old. Oh, Mrs. Holcomb died last year. She couldn't shake the cancer."

"I heard that. She was way too young."

"They didn't catch it soon enough. It just kind of appeared and got out of control. But she got to see her grandchild first."

"Wait, what?" I asked.

"Wichita Junior and Edna are getting married in a month. She wanted to wait to lose the baby weight."

"What? Wichita and Edna? And they had a

baby?"

Bobby grinned. "I know. The prom queen and the gamer. Rumor has it they've been secretly in love since elementary school, and she just didn't want anyone to know. She's proud of him now though."

"Good, he's a good guy."

"A good man now," Bobby agreed.

"What's the baby's name?"

"Serena."

"Pretty… Wait! Do you remember my last night in town when we saw Edna out by the lake and we couldn't figure out who she was with?"

"Yeah, Wichita Jr."

I laughed. "What else?"

"You hear about Doug?"

"Just that he dropped out of school. Is he in trouble?"

Bobby hesitated. "He's gone."

"Dead?"

Bobby shook his head. "We don't know. It was a while after he dropped out. I think... everyone says he'd gotten into drugs. They said he was dealing. One night, he just didn't come home."

I said nothing, staring out the window as we passed the tall, neon flag-posts of franchise restaurants and grocery stores.

"Anything else happen that night?"

Bobby hesitated. "No comets or meteors or anything," he said softly. But Bobby never could lie.

"There was an eclipse. Just a small one, lunar. But there was one."

I nodded, closing my eyes. "There's going to be another big eclipse in a week."

"I know."

The thought of the eclipse lingered in the car for a moment. Then I shook my head. "I'm sorry for Doug's parents. That's awful."

"They've been having a hard time," Bobby agreed.

"How's the harvest this year?"

Bobby frowned. "Not good. We didn't get much rain until the last few weeks. Corn's really shot up since, but it might not be enough."

"Wow, that's rare for Torrance."

When we turned onto the Torrance exit, I felt my heart speed up. I prepared myself for everything to have changed and also for nothing to have changed. There was a new McDonald's and a new Starbucks. There was even a new car wash. But overall, Torrance remained Torrance.

Same corn. Same big open sky. Same smell on the wind when I rolled down the window of the old truck. A smell I couldn't break down and name in its parts but which, quite simply, the smell of Torrance.

I closed my eyes, feeling the summer sun hot against my skin. The sun didn't shine like this in the city. It baked and crackled and blazed. But it didn't make you feel like this. Like it knew you by name and knew how to warm all the coldest places of your body and make you feel somehow less alone.

"Are you staying at yours or ours?" Bobby asked.

"Mine."

"You want me to drop you there first, or do you want to wait until after dinner?"

"After dinner," I said.

Dinner with the O'Malley family was always worth having. And it had been a long time since I'd had a true O'Malley meal. Everyone in the O'Malley family loved cooking, from Mrs. O'Malley to Bobby and most of his siblings.

Mr. and Mrs. O'Malley had not changed at all in the last four years. Mr. O'Malley remained as tall and as wiry and as steely as ever; Mrs. O'Malley just as red-faced, jovial, and stout as I remembered.

The children, though, had done more than enough changing for all of them. Little Martha now stood as tall as me. She had long hair and spoke in prim sentences full of advanced vocabulary. This did not stop her from racing against—and beating —her brothers.

The two younger O'Malley brothers resembled Bobby as a teenager, except with even more acne. The older two brothers looked much like their father, although James was thicker set and more muscular than John.

O'Malley family mealtimes were loud and busy and funny and long. After dinner ended and after I'd been hugged fiercely by all seven O'Malley family members, after I'd eaten steak and biscuits and soup and pie, after beers on the porch listening to the summer songs of the crickets, after laughter and words that passed by and around but never stuck, it was time for me to go home.

I left the O'Malley house before dark fell. Bobby drove me in the old truck. Even though we were next door neighbors, that meant something very different in Torrance than in the city.

When Bobby's truck slumped onto the gravel drive up to my house, I felt a moment of fear, fear that my breath would stop, that my heart would hammer, that my mind would shatter into those thousand meteorites.

But it didn't. Nothing at all happened. Except I felt a little sad.

Bobby lingered on the porch as the sun threatened, in rays of violent orange and pink, to abandon us.

"How are you holding up?" he asked.

"I'm good."

"Really?"

I looked at the burgundy door of the house, at the old swing, and took a breath. "I'm good," I repeated. "I wish Mercury were here."

"I know, he made it so long."

We were silent a moment.

"There's food in the fridge. Everything's all ready for you," he said.

"Thanks."

Bobby put his hand on my shoulder and smiled. "I'll see you tomorrow, Stell Bell."

I watched Bobby go from the porch. His truck disappeared into the last desperate gold of sunlight, a tempest of dirt in his trail. Like an earthbound comet.

The swing jostled in the wind as the chimes tolled. Closing my eyes, I could see my daddy. I could see him standing right where I now stood. That last night. When the gold light of meteors had made an angel of a man.

I opened my eyes and went inside.

I don't believe in ghosts, but I believe in haunted houses. Memories haunt them. Memories so good it aches. Memories so sweet that the present drowns itself, basking in those yesterdays. Everywhere there was Daddy.

My old bedroom sat bare. Everything had been moved to the O'Malley house a long time ago. I shut the blinds and lay in bed waiting for the night to pass.

Over the course of the next week, I must have visited or been visited by everyone in Torrance. There was Sheriff Donalee and Mrs. Donalee. There was Pastor Bob who smiled enthusiastically when I told him he could call me Stella. There were the Holcombs and the Wichitas and the Thorntons. I met Wichita Jr. and Edna's baby.

The visit I was most afraid to make, the one that threatened my fragile hold on Dr. Voorhies' pronouncements, was to the Carters. As a result, I visited them last.

The Carter house had always been too small for the Carters. It was a one story ranch near the center of town. I remembered Mrs. Carter as a woman with an exquisite lawn. Now, the grass was too long and overcome by weeds. What flowers remained appeared ill-kept and haphazard. The branches of the tree hung low to the ground. Patches of brown interspersed the green grass like hives.

The button of the doorbell appeared to have collapsed long ago. I knocked on the splotchy green door and waited.

The door opened to reveal a woman with frizzy gray hair and sunken eyes. "St-Katie."

"Stella is fine," I said. "I'm in town for a few days and thought I'd visit."

"Come in, come in." Mrs. Carter opened the door the rest of the way and ushered me into her home.

The smell of rotting flowers hit like a punch.

The people of Torrance tend to be particular about their houses. They are hospitable, but they are also aggressive about keeping a tidy home at all times. Most strive to be ready for visitors or guests at a moment's notice. Mrs. Carter clearly wasn't concerned with that anymore, or, if she was, she no longer possessed the ability to maintain it.

The living room, the hall, the kitchen, everywhere I looked, flowers in stale, murky water withered. The dried up petals formed a crunchy carpet beneath my feet as she led me to the couch.

She moved a pile of papers so I could sit down, and then she took the adjacent seat. She perched herself at the very edge of the chair, not really saying anything, as if unsure how these things were supposed to go.

"How's Dina?" I asked.

Dina was good. She was at college now. She liked it. She'd been home for….

"How's Derek?" I asked.

Derek was also good. He'd graduated college, gotten married and had a child. He did something with computers that Mrs. Carter didn't understand. I laughed and said I wouldn't understand either.

"How's Darren?" I asked.

Darren, too, was good. He was finishing his last year of college and had a job with an accounting firm lined up.

"And how's your husband?"

This little piece of town gossip had missed me. "He's gone," she said. "He left me after... after... Doug."

"I'm so sorry."

"He might be back. He just... he said he needed to get away from Torrance." Here, she shook her head. "But I don't see what's so bad about Torrance. You look at the rest of the world. All the crime. All the drugs. All the terrorism. Why would anyone want to leave Torrance? There's nothing dangerous about Torrance just because... just because..." She stopped, taking a long, wavering breath. "But you left, too. But you're back now, aren't you? Back to stay?"

I shook my head. "I start grad school soon." I told her where I'd go to school. It was in one of those far away cities.

Mrs. Carter pursed her lips, and an uncomfortable silence tightened between us. I fished around for something to say, but Mrs. Carter started talking again. "Doug's not like your parents."

"Right, I never..."

"Your parents disappeared. It was weird. It was strange. Everyone knows it wasn't natural. There was no reason in the world for them to disappear. Everyone says so. Everyone thinks it must have been something out of the ordinary—aliens or the Devil or just about anything. But everyone knows they wouldn't have gone if they didn't have to. Everyone knows they're dead."

The words didn't sting like one might expect them to. It was like she said. Everyone knew they were dead. Including me.

"My Doug was all mixed up," she said. "He was mixed up with all the wrong people. And he was always in arguments with everyone. With... with his father. With me. He's just run off. He did that sometimes. I don't know why everyone keeps sending these flowers. They... he's not dead. He'll be back. When he runs out of money, he'll be back."

I leaned forward. "Mrs. Carter," I said as softly as I could manage. "Can you tell me what happened to him?"

She shook her head, but she started talking anyway. "It was a normal night. Just one of those little eclipses, the kind that you can't even tell is happening. We went out to try and have a look, but the church steeple and the tree were in the way. Doug said he wanted a better look. So he went off. He went off, and we both saw the cigarette light. I called after him not to be gone too long and to put out the darn cigarette. We all knew what happened when he was gone. And we thought he'd been doing well. Working at the O'Malley Farm, spending time with the O'Malley boys. Such good boys. Not like him. Not like him at all. We'd been watching so closely. But what harm could come from walking down the block? What harm could come when he was just going right past the church? There couldn't have been any harm, none at all? There really… he didn't put out the cigarette." Mrs. Carter's words blurred together until they ran into each other and knocked against each other and her eyes swam with the memories, with that last image of her son and his cigarette.

"I'm sorry, Mrs. Carter."

"He'll be back. You'll see. You'll see."

I said nothing. After spending so long with Mrs. O'Malley, I would not, I could not, make false promises.

The silence tightened once more between us, but I thought she had something more to say. And she did.

"That night with your father, did you... did you happen to see anything?"

"Yes, but I doubt it was real."

"What did you see?" she asked. "Did you... did he... a golden light... like a cocoon... was it that? A golden cocoon... say it wasn't... please, say it wasn't."

I stared at Mrs. Carter. My throat tightened. My pulse quickened. A hand seemed to shake me from the base of my spine.

"Yes." I had to give her that much. "Yes. That's what I saw."

"That's not what I saw," Mrs. Carter said. "There wasn't any light. I didn't see it. And no matter what he says, my husband didn't see it neither. It's not real. He's alive. He's coming back. It was a trick of the light—that cocoon. And the sparks—just his cigarette."

"You should go visit Dina. Or Derek. Or Darren. I'm sure they'd all love to have you."

"No, I have to be here, when he gets back."

I didn't answer. My eyes lingered on the dozens of dead bouquets, their rancid smell thick in the air.

"Can I help you clear out these flowers?"

"No, no. No, I think I want to have a lie down. You should... yes, I need a lie down."

I got up from the sofa, and Mrs. Carter walked

me to the front door. "Lovely to see you, dear, lovely to see you." She practically forced me through the door.

I stood for a moment before the door, my heart quivering. The sun was high and it was bright and maybe if it wasn't golden, at least, it was yellow and hot and strong. And there was nothing to fear right now. Nothing to be afraid of.

Mrs. Carter was clearly upset, clearly off kilter. She needed help. I imagined what Dr. Voorhies would say to her. Something about the meeting of love and fear being the perfect canvas for the mind's most terrible masterpieces.

A laugh filled the street. The sound echoed off the buildings and the trees. Birds went flying from their perch on the steeple of the church down the block.

I realized it was my laugh.

I stopped at once, got in my car, and drove to the O'Malley house. I parked outside and went straight into the kitchen where I found Mrs. O'Malley and Martha cooking for dinner.

"Oh, Stella, dear," Mrs. O'Malley stopped talking when she saw my face.

"Give me something to do, please."

Mrs. O'Malley didn't miss a beat. She handed me a silver bowl. "These eggs need beating. Now, don't forget to do it just like I taught you. The whisks need to get underneath, so it gets good and circulated."

With gratitude, I took the bowl from her hands and did as she said.

It was a while yet before my pulse slowed and my breathing returned to normal. Mrs. Carter was clearly losing her mind, I forced myself to think when I had no other choice but to remember. Dr. Voorhies was the sane one. The brain is a powerful thing.

In spare moments, I did as the O'Malley family had asked. I walked my land. I walked the fields. I took the path Bobby and I had carved between our two houses. I sat beneath the tree. The star that my childhood self had carved was higher now than before. It was nearly on a level with my shoulders when I stood. Once, I even hauled my way all the way into the branches and found the place where we'd carved our names.

I hadn't climbed a tree in years, but I did that day. I hung in that branch like a small child, and it groaned beneath my weight. With a finger, I traced our initials in the bark. BO + SC FOREVER. All these years later, and nothing had changed. Or everything had changed. Absolutely everything. But some things were still the same. This carving on this tree was still the same.

And then the branch broke, and I toppled to the earth. I laughed and laughed at that.

I felt strong. I felt alive. I felt like Dr. Voorhies had been right in that moment. And from that tree, I ran.

I broke through the invisible line with bravado and joy. My feet rejoiced to touch Callahan land, and Callahan land rejoiced to touch my feet.

I strode all the way through the corn straight to the edge.

And then I arrived.

My laughter and my strength dried up in my veins. I stood on the edge of the crater where I'd watched my father dissolve in light. And once again, I felt my throat tighten, my pulse quicken. In my head, I heard Mrs. Carter's words again. In my mind, I saw the same light cocoon and Doug and his glowing cigarette and then he was whisked away into a firework of sparks.

~ 10 ~

EVERY NIGHT, I climbed into bed before the dark.

Bobby and I went on the drives of old. On one of the last nights, we stopped by the Shack, where I ordered a burger with everything, a strawberry shake, and a large fry, and Bobby ordered his burger with ketchup only, his large fry, and his chocolate shake.

Bobby drove us to the lake, where the same old picnic table sat under the same old tree by the same water that could almost be light.

The warm wind tried to blow away our napkins, and children played on the playground. And we slurped our shakes down to the last little crevice of whipped cream.

Bobby leaned across the table, his hands folded in front of him. "Stella, I have missed this so much."

"I have, too." I realized the words were true as soon as I uttered them. I'd missed all of it. I'd missed the sunlight and the trees, the lake and the Shack. I'd missed Mr. and Mrs. O'Malley and Martha and all the others. I'd missed the Holcombs and the Wichitas and the Donalees and the sounds of crickets and children playing and even the scratch of cornstalks on my skin. I'd missed the air here and the sky. And, most of all, I'd missed Bobby.

"Are you nervous about the eclipse?" he asked.

I closed my eyes. "I wasn't... That's not true. I was, but I was telling myself not to be. I saw a therapist out there who told me that what I saw couldn't be real. That it was all just the meeting of love and fear and the brain is mysterious, etcetera, etcetera, etcetera. But then... then I went and talked to Mrs. Carter."

Bobby waited for me to go on.

"She's... she's crazy, but what she described... it was just like what I saw that night."

"It could be a coincidence," Bobby said.

"I could believe that I'm crazy," I said quietly. "I certainly believe that Mrs. Carter is crazy. But that we're both crazy and saw the exact same thing when I told only you and Dr. Voorhies about what I saw?" I shook my head.

"Well, it wasn't exactly the same, though, was it?"

"What do you mean?"

"It was only a small lunar eclipse. There were no meteors involved. So, no meteors, no meteor monsters."

"Oh." I stared at him for a moment. I didn't know what to make of that. What he said made sense. "But the light…" I murmured.

"There's always a light. Alien abductions have a light. Near death experiences have a light. I'm not saying that you hallucinated here. I'm just saying that just because Mrs. Carter saw light, it doesn't mean it was the same light. It doesn't mean anything. Mrs. Carter is a… very broken woman."

I pushed back a strand of hair the wind kept blowing in front of my face. The sun felt so close right now with its exploding corona of orange and pink. Our Shack food wrappers lay empty before us. Bobby was right here, and everything he said made everything so much easier. Maybe I could go on pretending. Maybe I could go on insisting that Dr. Voorhies was right all along.

"Sun's setting," I said, and Bobby knew what that meant.

We got up, threw out our trash, and he drove me home.

The day before the solar eclipse, I told everyone two things. The first was that I felt sick. I don't think anyone believed me, but the town of Torrance was too polite to challenge me.

The second was that I'd come to a decision.

With the O'Malley family gathered around the living room, an O'Malley family meal warm in all our stomachs, with dogs yapping at crickets outside as sunset colors warned of the coming night, I stood in front of the family with all eyes on me.

"I've made my decision about the farm. I know that land has been in the Callahan family for generations, but I am just not a farmer. I am an astronomer, and that's not going to change." Everyone looked at me with such warmth. "I think my father would understand when I say that signing the Callahan farm to you would still be keeping it in the family. Because you are my family. And I'm sure now."

Mr. O'Malley leaned forward. "Stella, honey, you don't have to make the decision for keeps. We can always keep the contract going. Another six years, another ten. What if you get married? What if your husband is a farmer?"

I shook my head. "I'm not going to change my mind. I'm sure. I want you to have the farm. For keeps."

The family was silent for a moment. Mrs. O'Malley squeezed first Mr. O'Malley's hand then mine.

Then Mr. O'Malley opened the closet door, keyed a number into the old safe inside that closet, and he pulled out a contract written long ago.

"It's all here, then," he said, handing me a thick pile of papers and a pen. "Remember, sweetheart, that we are family. If you change your mind, you just come and talk to me. I'll understand."

I laughed and took the pen from him. "I'm not going to change my mind."

And with that, I turned to the last page of the document, and I signed my name. And thereby, the Callahan family farm was absorbed into the larger O'Malley farm, from now into forever. I would receive a significant chunk of money from the contract, enough to help me through grad school. I handed him the contract and the pen and smiled.

"How do you feel?" he asked me.

"Great," I said, but I glanced out the windows at a sky deeply tinged with violent warnings of the coming night. Mrs. Carter was crazy, I told myself. Dr. Voorhies was sane. Dr. Voorhies was right.

All the same, my throat tightened and my pulse hastened. "I need to be getting back home, though."

"Of course," Mr. O'Malley said with all the tenderness a stoic man could manage.

Bobby and I drove in silence to my house. Part of me wanted us to walk that long ago path one last time, but it was getting too late for such adventures now. I was already cutting it dangerously close.

The silence between us was warm like always. Safe and sunny and whole.

That evening, Bobby hugged me. "You know, I've always believed you," he said softly.

"I know."

And I went inside and shut all the blinds over all the windows in the house. I knew I wouldn't sleep that night. Or the next.

I sat on my bed, and I waited for the eclipse to come and go.

All through the night, I lay there, thinking of other nights and falling stars and trying to remember what my momma was like and actually remembering what my daddy was like. They would have loved the eclipse. I knew that. Nothing would have held them back from watching. I would love the eclipse. And I did love the eclipse. But I couldn't bear the thought of it, the threat of it.

That night, the golden light wrapped and rewrapped my father, over and over again. Like a skipping record in my mind.

As morning broke, the nighttime feeling dug its claws in and wouldn't let go. As light filtered through the curtains, I felt the eclipse coming.

I made breakfast. I ate breakfast. I washed the dishes. I tried to read. I couldn't. I went out and stood on the porch.

The dawn light suffused the corn-crusted world in a dull golden glow. It hid its threat.

It was coming soon. The moon was so close to the sun already.

A comet had taken my mother, a meteor my father, but a small eclipse had claimed Doug. And I'd read of other cases. Eclipses in which whole towns were swallowed up by history.

On the road, a speck appeared. The speck grew into Bobby's truck, and a few seconds later, Bobby, trailing clouds of dust, parked in front of the house.

Armed with coffee, he smiled as he joined me on the porch. "Thought you could use some coffee."

"Thought I could use some company, you mean."

"That too," he said as I took the coffee. "Was I wrong?"

"I could use both." I smiled

"Hold on a sec." He set his own coffee down on the porch's railing. He went back to his truck and returned with two pairs of protective glasses. "Here, just in case you wanted to see."

"Fat chance." I glanced worriedly at the sky. "I'm going inside."

Inside, we drank our coffee and we talked of nothing and we waited.

There came a time when the morning light began to dim. I closed my eyes and clutched my coffee.

Bobby looked wistfully at the window.

I frowned. "You can go look. Just... just be careful. And stay on the porch... Please."

Bobby stood up and crossed to me. He knelt and pressed a kiss on the top of my head. "I'll be fine. I'll just look real quick and come back in."

I watched Bobby open the door.

I saw night outside.

Bobby closed the door, and I rose to my feet. I put the coffee aside and walked to the front door. I put my back against the wood and listened.

In a rush of motion, without thinking or hesitating, I opened the door and forced myself onto the porch.

Night was fallen, the moon's path nearly complete. The sun burned an outraged orange like the pit of a volcano or the core of the world.

Bobby turned to me and smiled as I stood beside him on the porch, pressing my shoulder into his.

"You couldn't let me face it alone," he said softly, putting his hand on top of mine.

My head nodded.

He smiled. "You always were so brave."

I didn't feel brave, but I put on the glasses. And I looked.

I could see the moon moving. The orange cast to the darkness soaked the world in the shadows of hellfire.

And then the moon finished its path.

The orange light of the sun blazed out from behind the pitch black core. It was like gazing at something secret, at once profound and profane.

My hand squeezed Bobby's.

"It's okay," he whispered, his other hand on my cheek, turning my face toward him. He resembled the Bobby he used to be in these strange glasses. I could see all the nights in his eyes. All the drives and the days and the climbed trees and the copied homework and the silences and the words.

"My Stella Bell is starlight hiding from the stars. My Stella Bell is starlight as a girl. She walks and she talks and she laughs all the places she has seen— all the galaxies and supernovas and black holes in between. My Stella Bell is a star a billion years ago.

My Stella Bell is a girl right here and right now. She doesn't know it and she never will, but I love my Stella Bell," he said softly. "That was the real poem from that night in the park before…"

And I leaned in and kissed him.

My daddy was right after all.

Through my closed eyes, I saw a brightening. Through the kiss, I knew the eclipse was ending. Safety was coming.

I opened my eyes.

The light did not come from the sky. The light came from the chrysalis surrounding me.

Bobby took a step back from me, a sad smile on his face. "You always thought it was the cosmos," he said softly, his hand still on my face. "In a way, it is. We did come to earth that way. We came as stars. But comets and eclipses are just our cover now. After your momma, my momma thought it would be poetic if we only did it when the cosmos winked."

The light became brighter and brighter around me. I knew it surrounded my entire body now. I saw myself from a distance the way I'd once seen my father.

"What are you?" I whispered.

Bobby shrugged. "It's just as I told you that first night. We're gods. We keep the corn growing, the sun shining, the people kind. We create your perfect world of Torrance. We just need sacrifice to keep it going."

"Why us?" I asked.

"We take the brightest lights," he said. "Your mother with her fiery spirit. Your father with his fierce love. Even Doug Carter with his wild heart. But it turns out, Doug Carter was not enough to fix what is plaguing Torrance."

"You mean, the lack of rain?"

"And Mrs. Holcomb's cancer," Bobby said slowly. "Taking Doug got us some rain, but not enough. And Mrs. Holcomb still died."

He smiled at me so very sadly, his brown eyes now more like flaming meteors than river mud. "So now here we are. You and me. And you, with the soul of a star. I really do love you, my Stella Bell. We always do love the ones we take."

He leaned in and placed one last kiss on my lips.

And then everything turned to golden light.

One thing about the women of Torrance, Indiana. We know how to shoot.

I pulled Daddy's pistol from the waistband of my jeans where I'd put it the moment I got it out of the safe my first night back.

I pressed the muzzle to his heart. And I pulled the trigger.

The shot shattered the strange symphony of light.

The light went out, the eclipse still gazing on from above.

Bobby O'Malley collapsed, a faint light still glimmering in his eyes. "My Stella Bell. You always were the real star in town."

Then that golden cocoon surrounded him. And it was Bobby O'Malley, murderer of my momma and my daddy and Doug Carter, who exploded into a cascade of golden fireworks illuminating the darkness.

As that light faded, there came seven more flashes. One after the other. As if all eight of these O'Malley creatures were bound together as one.

And as the last flash ended, the moon edged away from the sun, lifting the darkness from over Torrance.

We had a very good harvest that year indeed.

ABOUT THE AUTHOR

Josh Dygert's short stories have appeared in a number of online magazines and anthologies, including in the #1 Amazon Bestselling Horror Anthology *Secret Stairs.* He is also the author of a middle-grade fantasy novel called *The Story Traveler,* which is available from Amazon. He studied English and Theater in college and now teaches middle school English. He can be found online at joshdygert.com.

CPSIA information can be obtained
at www.ICGtesting.com
Printed in the USA
LVHW041927020720
659557LV00003B/210